A NORTH-SOUTH PAPERBACK

Critical praise for
Rinaldo on the Run

"Children who love the traditional trickery of Renard . . .
are sure to enjoy this more modern and sophisticated
adventure. . . . Charming cartoon animals and amusing
details . . . plus the action-packed slapstick humor make
this title a winner." *School Library Journal*

"These light-hearted adventures offer beginning readers
just enough action and comical situations to keep their
interest and woo them on to the next installment."
Children's Book Review

Rinaldo
on the Run

by Ursel Scheffler

PICTURES BY

Iskender Gider

Translated by J. Alison James

North-South Books

NEW YORK / LONDON

First published in the United States, Great Britain, Canada,
Australia, and New Zealand in 1995 by North-South Books,
an imprint of Nord-Süd Verlag AG, Gossau Zürich, Switzerland.
First paperback edition published in 1996.
Distributed in the United States by North-South Books Inc., New York.

Library of Congress Cataloging-in-Publication Data
Scheffler, Ursel.
[Schlaue Fuchs Rinaldo als Pizza-Konig. English]
Rinaldo on the run / by Ursel Scheffler ; pictures by Iskender Gider ; translated by J. Alison James.
Summary: After a clever cat steals his fortune and his fancy sports car,
Rinaldo, the sly fox, travels to Rome and then to visit his long-lost uncle Dusty,
the Pizza King, in America, while trying to avoid his nemesis, Bruno the duck detective.
[1. Foxes—Fiction. 2. Ducks—Fiction. 3. Criminals—Fiction.
4. Animals—Fiction.] I. Gider, Iskender, Ill. II. James, J. Alison. III. Title.
PZ7.S3425Rg 1995 94-42453
A CIP catalogue record for this book is available from The British Library.
For more information about our books, and the authors and artists who create them, visit our web site:
http://www.northsouth.com

ISBN 1-55858-405-6 (TRADE BINDING)
1 3 5 7 9 TB 10 8 6 4 2
ISBN 1-55858-406-4 (LIBRARY BINDING)
1 3 5 7 9 LB 10 8 6 4 2
ISBN 1-55858-622-9 (PAPERBACK)
1 3 5 7 9 PB 10 8 6 4 2
Printed in Belgium

Contents

Bruno the Duck Sees Red

"Whaaat! You let Rinaldo get away?"

Bruno the Duck Detective waved the wanted poster in the air. "You saw him and did not bring him in?"

"I'm afraid so," said the guard. "We didn't recognize him. He was going by the name Rinaldo Richman and driving a fancy red sports car with a lovely cat in the passenger seat."

"The phony swindler!" blustered Bruno, "The rogue, the rascal, the scoundrel, the villain! I'm going to catch him and make mincemeat out of him. Do you have any idea where he went?"

"He asked about the fastest way to Feathertown," said the guard.

"Aha!" Bruno cried. "He knows I'm out on his trail, so he's going to sneak back to town while I'm away. I'll have to go straight back and protect the henhouses!" He roared away on his hot red motorcycle.

Rinaldo Strays from the Straight and Narrow

Of course Rinaldo had never planned to go near Feathertown. He also hadn't planned to lose his fancy car, his fortune, or his lovely cat companion. But there he was, alone and penniless, at the edge of the dusty road, trying to hitch a ride to Rome. Car after car roared past. Finally someone stopped.

The driver leaned out of the window and asked, "Where you headed?"

"Rome," answered Rinaldo, eagerly eyeing the picture of a delicious-looking hen on the side of the truck.

"Climb in," said the man. "I'm Carlo Muli. I just dropped off a load of chickens in Milan and am going back to Rome to pick up a new load."

"No chickens? Too bad," said Rinaldo.

"I don't care—just as long as I get paid," said the driver, tapping his money bag. "Here, have some of my sandwich."

"Thanks," said Rinaldo. "And thanks for the ride. I was desperate. A few days ago, I was robbed by a cat."

"A cat? How could that happen to a fox like you?"

"She was a real cat burglar! She took my keys and drove off with my car and everything I owned."

"I'm sorry to hear that," said Muli. "It sure is a tough world out there. You have to look out for yourself."

At the next rest area, Muli pulled off
and said, "I'll be back in a minute. Would
you keep an eye on my money bag?"

"I won't take my eyes off it," promised
Rinaldo. And he didn't.

As soon as Muli disappeared, Rinaldo
quickly tied a string to the money bag,
tucked the string out of sight, and put the
bag back exactly where it had been. "Just
in case of an emergency," he thought.

When Muli returned, he looked carefully at Rinaldo, then smiled. "Why don't you climb in the back and take a little snooze?"

Rinaldo climbed in the back, but he only pretended to sleep. He heard the driver chuckling to himself: "Stupid fox! Didn't he think I'd see the wanted poster? When he wakes up, we'll be at the police station and I'll turn him in for the reward money."

"I guess this counts as an emergency," said Rinaldo as he pulled the string and reeled in Muli's money bag.

When Muli stopped at a light, Rinaldo slipped out of the back.

He found a sunny spot at a little café and ordered something to eat. When he looked in the money bag, his heart beat with joy. He was penniless no more.

The café was in a charming little coastal
town, so Rinaldo decided to stay for a
holiday. As he was taking a walk along the
beach, the scent of the fishing boats hit
him in the nose. It reminded him of his
arch enemy, Bruno the Duck Detective. "I

think a little gift is in order," he said to
himself.

"Won't Bruno be surprised! I bet he
can't wait to rip into this!" thought
Rinaldo as he carried the tightly sealed
package to the post office.

Bruno Gets
a Breath of Sea Air

Bruno the Duck stood in his kitchen, peeling potatoes. He was furious. Rinaldo still had not arrived in Feathertown. Bruno had been outsmarted again!

Someone knocked on the door.

"A package for you, Bruno. Express mail from Rome!"

"For me?" cried Bruno, surprised. "But my birthday is not until next month."

The package was carefully wrapped.

The card read:

Greetings from the Mediterranean Sea!
Feathertown is where I would rather be.
I'm still free, you're out of luck.
Happy birthday, you foolish duck!

The card was unsigned, and Bruno was suspicious. Warily he inspected the package from all sides.

"What if a bomb is inside?" he thought.

He tested the package with his bomb detector. Nothing. Could it really be a completely normal birthday package?

Bruno cut the tape. Then he ripped off the paper. Then he opened the box. Yeech! Out of the box came a hideous stench. It was fish, rotten fish, rotten starfish and mussels and squid.

The Duck sizzled with fury. "This time the scoundrel has gone too far! I won't rest until I catch him!" Bruno took off at a run, slipped on a potato, tripped over the coal skuttle, and broke his left leg.

Two orderlies carried Bruno to the
Feathertown hospital. While a doctor
wrapped his leg in plaster, Bruno clamped
his beak shut. He appeared very cool on
the outside. But inside he was seething.
"Just you wait," he growled. "As soon as I
can hobble away from here, I'll be on your
heels. And in the meantime, I'll set my
colleague Malefizio Colombo on your tail."
And he sent a fax with Rinaldo's photo off
to Rome.

Rinaldo Gets Out of a Hot Spot

Rome is a real hot spot. Especially in summer. Especially if you are running from the police. And most especially if, like Rinaldo, you are running from the police dressed in a monk's robes. Since Rome is full of monks, Rinaldo thought the robe would be a good disguise. But while he was having dinner, he noticed a fellow at the next table reading the paper. Rinaldo took a peek. There was his photo!

His ice cream stuck in his throat. They were searching for him all over Italy! Confound it, Bruno hadn't even bothered to come himself, but set the Italian police after him. And there they were!

Rinaldo ducked into his hood. The police glanced around—and went on by. What luck!

Rinaldo's disguise may have saved him this time, but a monk without a monastery couldn't fool the police for long. What could he do?

Rinaldo stared at his empty pizza plate. The Sly Fox he saw reflected there reminded him of his uncle Dusty, who had started a pizza company in America. Now he had ninety-seven franchises. He must be a millionaire! Why not stir up a little dust and go to Chicago to visit his uncle Dusty, the Pizza King?

Rinaldo bought a briefcase, a pinstripe suit, and big sunglasses.

That very afternoon, dressed as a businessman, he stepped aboard a jet bound for Chicago.

Bruno, the Duck Detective, was hot on Rinaldo's trail. He hobbled to Rome just in time to watch the Sly Fox disappear into the blue sky.

"Outfoxed again!" moaned Bruno, and
bit his hat in fury.

Rinaldo
Feathers His Own Nest

Dustin Polecat, the Pizza King, was thrilled to see Rinaldo. "A nephew!" he exclaimed. "How wonderful! I didn't know I had any relatives. Now I finally have someone who can inherit my fortune! You must learn the business. Start at the bottom as a pizza baker, just as I did. 'All work, no play,' I always say."

"I'm very sensitive to heat," Rinaldo protested. "But if you need any advice about money, I have lots of experience."

So Rinaldo became Uncle Dusty's accountant.

He carefully checked his Uncle's books.

"You certainly have enough money," said Rinaldo happily.

"It will all be yours one day," said Dusty.

"Don't talk like that," said Rinaldo. "I'm not thinking about your money, I'm thinking about you. You won't last much longer unless you take better care of yourself. You're looking rather pale."

"Do you think so?" asked Dusty,
shocked. He turned a little paler.

Rinaldo looked worried.

"Oh, dear!" cried Dusty after an anxious
glance in the mirror. "You are absolutely
right. I look pale as a ghost. Do you think
I'm going to die?"

"Don't be silly. You have just been working too hard. What you need is a holiday. Take a few weeks in Hawaii—a complete rest. Nobody will be able to reach you. I'll keep it a secret. When you come back, you will feel like you've started a new life. I guarantee it!"

"Perhaps you're right," said Dusty. "But who will collect the money from the franchises while I'm gone?"

"That is why you hired me!" said Rinaldo.

"Oh, thank you, Nephew. You are too good to me," said Dusty. "I'll always remember you for this."

"I'm sure you will," replied Rinaldo.

The next morning Rinaldo took his uncle to the airport. That afternoon he told everyone that the Pizza King was quite sick, and that he, Rinaldo, would be taking over for him.

Each night, he sat at Uncle Dusty's desk and collected the money from the ninety-seven pizza franchises. When the managers asked about Uncle Dusty, Rinaldo would shake his head sadly.

After seven days Rinaldo put on his pinstripe suit, knotted a tie, and informed everyone that poor Uncle Dusty had died. He ordered music and flowers for the funeral.

None of the mourners noticed that instead of Uncle Dusty's body, there were heavy stones in the coffin. As for Uncle Dusty, he was having the time of his life on the beach at Waikiki.

The day before Uncle Dusty was supposed to return, Rinaldo packed his bags. They were a lot heavier than they had been on the trip *to* Chicago. Rinaldo left a note on the table:

Dear Uncle Dusty,

Welcome back! Just as I promised, you will feel you are beginning a new life! I've kept the secret . . . all the way to the grave.

Yours truly,

Rinaldo

Rinaldo Makes a First Class Acquaintance

Rinaldo leaned back happily in the plush, wide seat. It was great to be able to afford a first-class ticket. To start off, he had a glass of chilled raspberry juice. He asked the stunning bird in the seat beside him if she would like to help him celebrate his great business success. Her name was Riki Goldpheasant, and she was returning from a week-long fashion show in New York. She had been launching a line of new clothes, and was exhausted.

"You won't believe how much I am looking forward to a peaceful weekend in the country," Riki said.

"Me too," said Rinaldo, and he yawned. "I think I'll treat myself to a long holiday."

"Was your trip really that successful?"

"You could say that." Rinaldo smiled cunningly. "Would you like to take a peek in my briefcase?"

He lifted the lid of his burgundy briefcase and let his companion take a look.

"Oh my! That is quite something!" said Riki when she caught sight of the bundles of cash. She looked at Rinaldo with wide, admiring eyes.

After they had had dinner, Riki got very quiet.

So Rinaldo took a nap.

Time flew by. Shortly after breakfast, the pilot said, "We are starting our descent into Foolscop. Please fasten your seat belts."

"Excuse me," said Riki Goldpheasant. "I just need to go to the ladies."

"I'm sure there is time for that," said Rinaldo, glancing out of the window. "We are still above the clouds."

Rinaldo Lands in Trouble

Riki Goldpheasant went to the flight attendant. She showed him her Special Agent of the International Police ID.

"I have to make a telephone call!" she whispered. "A dangerous criminal is on board: Mascapone the Blackmailer."

The flight attendant turned pale. "Are you quite certain?" he asked.

Agent Goldpheasant nodded.

"We must inform the captain right away," said the flight attendant.

Quickly they slipped into the cockpit.

"We had a tip that he would be aboard this flight, carrying a burgundy briefcase." Riki told them. "But we didn't know what name he would be using, or how he'd be disguised. Fortunately, I have unmasked him!"

"Are you quite certain?" asked the captain.

43

Agent Goldpheasant nodded. "I saw the case with the money in it myself. Thick bundles of hundred-dollar bills."

"Then we must inform the police immediately!" declared the captain. He radioed the airport police with the exciting news. They asked him to circle a few more times so they could get ready to catch the criminal.

The passengers on board became impatient. "What is happening?" asked a nervous passenger. His name was Willie Wolf, and his burgundy briefcase looked exactly like Rinaldo's.

Finally the captain announced on the loud speakers: "We have to circle for a few minutes more. We're fourth in line to land now."

Rinaldo was relaxed and easygoing.

"What does it matter if we're a few minutes late? Nobody is expecting me. My arrival is supposed to be a surprise."

"I hope that the surprise is successful," Riki said cheerfully.

The plane started its descent and in a few minutes landed on the runway.

"What on earth is going on?" exclaimed Rinaldo as he looked out of the window. "There are police all over the place!"

"Probably some dignitary on the plane," said Riki lightly.

Rinaldo picked up his case with a flourish. "I guess that's what happens when you fly first class. Let's be on our way," he said to Riki.

And whistling, he followed her straight down the aisle, straight down the steps, and straight into the arms of the police.

Rinaldo Gets Good News—and Bad News

Rinaldo was held for questioning at the police station. "I am not Mascapone!" he said again and again. "Honest!"

"Who are you, then?" asked Commissioner Mouse.

"We've found passports under three different names in your luggage. Are you Rinaldo, Grimaldo, Rinaldini, or what?"

"My name is Rinaldo Grimaldo Rinaldini. One name is for my father, one for my grandfather, and one for my great-grandfather. Some days I like one name better than the others. . . ."

"So that's your story. Well, we have other ways to learn the truth. We have sent an inquiry to Feathertown. Number 4 Peapod Street. Recognize the address? It was on a receipt for an express-mail package that we found in your briefcase."

"It is just—ah, just the address of a special friend," said Rinaldo, and ice-cold shivers ran up his back.

"A friend? Good. If this friend confirms that you are Rinaldo Grimaldo Rinaldini and not Mascapone, then you'll be on your way," said the Mouse.

"I'll be on my way, all right," thought Rinaldo grimly as he sat in his cell. "On my way to the Feathertown jail." But if Commissioner Mouse didn't reach Bruno the Duck, they would keep him in the Foolscop jail, thinking that he was this terrible Mascapone!

Either way, Rinaldo was stuck, stuck in a cell with a briefcase full of money he couldn't spend. It was unbearable.

Rinaldo looked around. The window was barred. Outside the door stood two strong policemen. It wouldn't be easy to catch them off guard.

No, for the moment he was trapped.

Next door, in the Mouse's office, the phone rang. The Commissioner said, "Hello?" He listened, amazed. First his brow crinkled with anger; then he smiled slyly.

When he came to see Rinaldo, he said, "I have good news and bad news. Which would you like first?"

"The good, I guess," said Rinaldo with a sigh.

"The blackmailer's real name is Willie Wolf. So it's not you."

Rinaldo sat up and grinned. "Didn't I tell you? Nobody would believe me!" he said. "I demand that you release me immediately. And as for this, this, Riki Goldpheasant, I have another hen to pluck with her."

"Not before you hear the bad news," said Commissioner Mouse. "You are wanted for robbery, fraud, escaping from prison, insulting the police, and a long list of other things. My colleague Bruno the Duck Detective is on his way here."

Rinaldo's goose was cooked.

Bruno Dreams of Glory

"Ha! At last I've got you, you old swindler!" cried Bruno the Duck. He was delighted to find Rinaldo looking so sad and defeated in jail. "This time we won't take any chances: March straight to the van! Off to Feathertown we go!" He pointed his peashooter and shoved Rinaldo into his spinach-green lock-up van.

Rinaldo's legs were shackled.

The Duck tied him to a heavy tool chest. Then he locked the van door with three separate locks. Bruno put the keys in his pocket.

"This time he will not escape!" said Bruno the Duck triumphantly as he sat behind the wheel.

All the way back, Bruno dreamed of the headlines in the paper:

RINALDO BEHIND BARS! BRUNO THE DUCK—HERO OF THE DAY!

With his photo on the front page! He would send a copy to his friend Lili Downy. How proud she would be of him. They would make a toast: "To Bruno, the courageous, diligent Duck Detective!"

But good luck breaks as easily as good glass. While Bruno victoriously drove his green van along the highway, Rinaldo, the Sly Fox, saw an escape from his seemingly hopeless situation.

It was a little tricky, but as Uncle Dusty used to say, "All work, no play."

About the Illustrator

Iskender Gider was born in Istanbul, Turkey.
When he was nine years old, he moved with
his parents to Germany, where he went to
school in Cologne and Recklinghausen.
Today he is a commercial artist and an
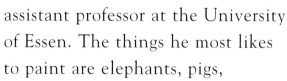 assistant professor at the University
of Essen. The things he most likes
to paint are elephants, pigs,
chickens, and foxes—
especially sly foxes like
Rinaldo.

About the Author

Ursel Scheffler was born in Nuremberg,
a German city where many toys are made.
She has written over one hundred children's
books, which have been published in fifteen
different languages. She has a special liking
for foxes and other two- and four-legged
tricksters—as you can
see from this story.

Don't miss the first two book in this series:

Rinaldo, the Sly Fox
The Return of Rinaldo, the Sly Fox

Available from North-South Books